THE ADVENTURES OF
DR. BRAIN
& MR. STRONG

D1307806

Copyright Elnoir Jane Publishing/Lashandra Hall. All rights reserved. Printed in the United States of America. No part of this book may be used or reproduced in any manner whatsoever without written permission except in the case of brief quotations embodies in critical articles and reviews. This is a work of fiction. Names, characters, places and incidents are either the product of the author's imagination or are used fictitiously, and any resemblance to actual persons, living or dead, business establishments, events or locals is entirely coincidental. If you purchased this book without a cover you should be aware that this book is stolen property. It was reported as "unsold and destroyed" to the publisher, and neither the author nor the publisher has received any payment for this "stripped" book. Quantity sales and special discounts are available on quantity purchases by corporations, associations, and others. For details, contact Elnoir Jane Publishing via email lashandramhall@gmail.com or visit www.lashandrahall.com.

Library of Congress has been applied for.

Copyright © 2017 Elnoir Jane Publishing
Lashandra Hall
ISBN-13: 978-1976189388

Acknowledgements

Thank you to all the people who have made this

book possible. I am forever grateful for your hard

work and diligence.

AJ and Baby JD this one is for you!

Love you forever.

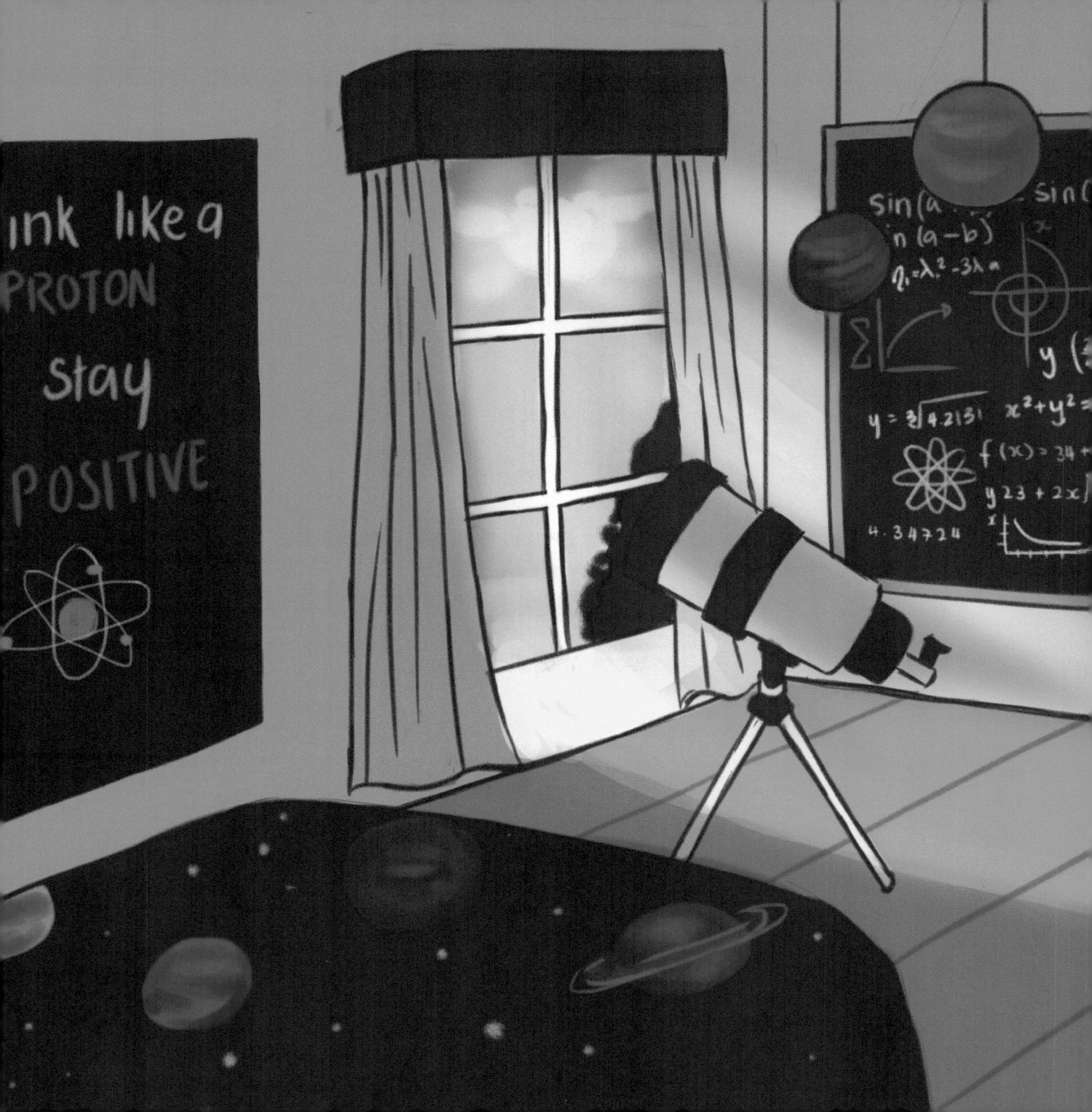
ink like a
PROTON
stay
POSITIVE
y = 3√4.2131
4.34724

There once was a boy who had thing,
for being the smartest. He had smart dreams.

Dreams of math.

Dreams of science.

He loved to make potions

and fill his brain with knowledge.

He wore a white coat and thin black glasses.
He carried pens in his pocket and pictures of the
planet.

He was quirky. Some called him strange.
He was a scholar who did nothing the same.

He had a buddy he never could find, until it was time to show his mind.

He stayed silent until he was needed.
He never spoke a word and didn't like for
anyone to see him.

He liked to hide
and pop up with flare.

He was huge and quick. Catch him if you dare.

His brain was big and he was strong as an ox.

He could run through walls head first, nonstop.

He learned so much
by the age of two.

Ask him anything the
answer he knew.

He was fast as a rabbit
and he loved to play.

He had a thing for blue
candy and carrot cake.

They were two boys who were completely opposite.

When they put their brains together they were unstoppable.

They put out huge fires.

They saved cats from trees.

They carried little girls books

and helped little ladie cross the street.

They worked around the clock

doing good deeds.

They were rewarded with cake and huge kisses on the cheek.

They worked day and night and never missed school.

They always made it home for supper, their moms were fooled.

They had no idea their boys were heroes.

They kept it a secret.
They liked to be incognito.

Everyone loved them and the way they get along.

the world of

MR. STRONG

CPSIA information can be obtained
at www.ICGtesting.com
Printed in the USA
LVHW072306201118
597793LV00014B/326/P